The Sontaran Games

The Sontaran Games

Jacqueline Rayner

2 4 6 8 10 9 7 5 3 1

Published in 2009 by BBC Books, an imprint of Ebury Publishing.
Ebury Publishing is a division of the Random House Group Ltd.

© Jacqueline Rayner, 2009
Jacqueline Rayner has asserted her right to be identified as the author
of this Work in accordance with the Copyright, Design and Patents Act
1988.

Doctor Who is a BBC Wales production for BBC One
Executive Producers: Russell T Davies and Julie Gardner

Original series broadcast on BBC Television. Format © BBC 1963.
'Doctor Who', 'TARDIS' and the Doctor Who logo are trademarks of the
British Broadcasting Corporation and are used under licence. Sontarans
created by Robert Holmes. Rutans created by Terrance Dicks.

The Random House Group Ltd Reg. No. 954009.
Addresses for companies within the Random House Group can be found
at www.randomhouse.co.uk.

A CIP catalogue record for this book is available from the British Library.

ISBN 978 1 846 07643 5

The Random House Group Limited supports the Forest Stewardship
Council (FSC), the leading international forest certification organisation.
All our titles that are printed on Greenpeace approved FSC certified
paper carry the FSC logo. Our paper procurement policy can be found
at www.rbooks.co.uk/environment

Series Consultant: Justin Richards
Project Editor: Steve Tribe
Cover design by Lee Binding © BBC 2009

Typeset in Stone Serif
Printed and bound in Great Britain by
CPI Cox & Wyman, Reading, RG1 8EX

The Sontaran Games

Chapter One

The room was briefly lit up as the Doctor left the TARDIS. Then he shut the doors of his time machine behind him, and the room became dark again.

The Doctor started to walk forward, but stumbled. He pulled a torch out of his pocket and switched it on. Pointing the beam at his feet, he looked to see what had tripped him up. There on the ground was a pair of thick rubber boots and what looked like a toolbox.

He raised the torch, and a pale face screamed out of the blackness at him.

The Doctor barked in surprise, sounding like a startled seal. The torch beam wobbled for a moment as he stepped backwards. Then he laughed in relief, as he saw that this was no deadly alien – it was just a young woman. She was wearing a swimming costume, which seemed strange to the Doctor, as it was obviously the middle of the night. But then perhaps on this planet his blue suit, brown coat and trainers would look odd.

'Where did you come from?' he asked the young woman. 'There was no one here a minute ago!' Then he remembered his manners, and added, 'I'm sorry I scared you.'

She didn't answer, just asked him the same question. 'Where did *you* come from?'

'Just now? Oh, the planet Pootle,' the Doctor replied. He waved his hand in the air to indicate somewhere a long way off. The light from the torch bounced around the room as he did so. 'Ever been there?'

She stared at him for a moment and finally said, 'No.'

'Lovely beaches, but the sharks are deadly. As in, three metres tall with guns. So I made a quick getaway and ended up here, in your lovely, er, house.'

'You mean BASE,' the girl said.

'Base? Like an army base? Base camp?'

'No, this is BASE. The British Academy of Sporting Excellence.'

The Doctor screwed up his face. '*British*? So, I'm on Earth?'

'Yes,' she replied, earning a giant grin from the Doctor.

'Great! I love Earth!'

'Mm. Me too,' said the young woman. She was giving the Doctor an odd look. There again,

2

he thought, it might just be an effect of the torchlight.

From somewhere to the left of the Doctor came the sound of a door opening. He swung the torch round, making the young man who'd entered fling up a hand to shield his eyes. The youth blinked a few times, then squinted ahead. 'Oh, it's you, Emma,' he said, sounding annoyed. 'What was all that yelling and screaming about? After what happened to Laura and the others...'

'I can look after myself, Sid,' the girl replied. 'Nothing's going to happen to me.'

'I don't expect Laura thought anything was going to happen to her either,' the young man began. He stopped speaking when, with a pop, a light came on. A soft yellow glow from an overhead bulb suddenly bathed the room.

'Oh, well done,' said Sid, turning to the Doctor. 'You've sorted it!'

The Doctor glanced over his shoulder, just in case the young man was speaking to someone else. He shrugged as he put the torch back in his pocket. 'It wasn't me,' he said.

'You're not an electrician?' Sid looked at the toolbox by the Doctor's feet.

'Nope.' The Doctor grinned. 'I'm the Doctor, you're Sid and I take it this is Emma.' He turned

3

to the girl. 'And I would really like to know what happened to Laura and the others...'

Sid led the way out of the room. The Doctor had dodged questions about the large blue box that was now standing there. He didn't want to waste time trying to explain that the box was really his spaceship. He just wanted to hear Sid and Emma's tale.

BASE, he discovered, was a training ground for gifted athletes. All of the young people who lived there were hoping to be chosen for the Globe Games. This was a huge new sporting contest. Teams from every continent in the world would compete in track and field events, swimming, gymnastics, weightlifting and more. It seemed that anything that allowed one human being to prove himself best in a contest of speed, strength or skill was included.

Sid was a javelin thrower and Emma, as the Doctor guessed, was a swimmer. Laura had been a swimmer too.

'We're only supposed to train during the day,' Sid told the Doctor. 'A lot of people do some sneaky practice after the coaches have gone home, though. Anything to get an edge on the others. Only a few of us will be chosen to go to the Games, so there's a lot of rivalry. We think that's why Laura had gone to the pool that night.' A sad look crossed his face. 'It was only a week ago. It seems like for ever. She was found there the next morning, in the water. Dead.' He bit his lip. 'That's why I was worried when I heard Emma scream tonight.'

The Doctor looked from one to the other. 'Why? Is someone bumping off all the swimmers?'

Emma shook her head. 'He means because of the power cut. The first one was that night, the night Laura died. And since then, every time the power's gone out—'

'Someone has died,' Sid finished.

'Three people so far,' added Emma. 'Laura, a sprinter called Joe, and Andy, a discus thrower.'

The Doctor stared at them, amazed. 'You're telling me that athletes are dropping like flies whenever the lights go out? Why isn't the place crawling with police? Come to that, why haven't you all gone home?'

Sid wouldn't meet the Doctor's eyes. 'Well, there's a lot at stake here, you know,' he mumbled. 'They're going to be picking the teams soon.'

The Doctor raised his eyebrows. 'You're worried that an inquiry might stop you being chosen for some big egg-and-spoon race. So you're hushing up three fishy deaths?'

Sid and Emma both looked at the floor.

The Doctor grinned. 'Well, at least there won't be anyone getting in my way while I look into it, then, will there?'

Chapter Two

The coaches didn't live at BASE. Only the students stayed there full time, and they weren't supposed to leave the complex. Contact with family and friends was forbidden. The training was tough, and it wasn't unknown for athletes to drop out without warning. That was how the rest of the students had kept anyone from finding out about the deaths.

'Did you really think you'd get away with it?' the Doctor asked in disgust. He looked down at the three lifeless bodies. They had been locked in a disused changing room, laid out on wooden benches. 'These were people, real people. People who loved them are going to come looking, in the end.'

Sid gritted his teeth. 'Their families would understand,' he said. 'They know what a big deal the Games are.'

The Doctor opened his mouth, but the words stopped when he saw Emma's face.

'I... I didn't think,' she said. 'I just went along with it. I hadn't... I hadn't seen any of them.' She pointed towards one of the benches, turning her face away, so she wasn't looking at the body. It was still dressed in a red swimming costume. 'That's Laura.' She gave a half-smile. 'My biggest rival. I think I miss her. Maybe she wasn't such a bad person after all.'

The Doctor held out a hand to her, and led her back out of the changing room. Sid followed. 'You two stay here,' he said, his voice much softer now. 'I'll be out in a minute.'

It was more like twenty minutes before the Doctor joined Emma and Sid in the corridor. They weren't looking at each other. There was clearly no love lost between them. Emma was sitting cross-legged on the floor. She jumped up when the door opened, looking scared.

'Well?' said Sid. 'What happened to them?'

'They were electrocuted,' the Doctor said.

Sid looked puzzled.

'Zap!' went the Doctor, in case the youth hadn't understood. 'A thousand volts, zzzzzz, ow! Water and electricity don't mix. Don't take a toaster in the bath, however peckish you're feeling.'

'You mean it was something in the swimming pool?' Emma asked. 'An accident?'

The Doctor raised an eyebrow. 'Oh no. No

accident. I found burns on the other two because there was no water to spread the current around. There's something very odd going on here. So, who do you think wants to win so much that they'd commit murder?'

Sid gaped at him. 'Murder?'

'Could be.'

The young man shrugged his shoulders. 'Now you mention it, it wouldn't really be a big surprise. So, what were you doing roaming around at night, Emma?'

Emma gasped. 'Me? What about you? Anyway, that doesn't make sense. All the victims did different sports. If they'd all been swimmers you might be on to something, but they weren't.'

The Doctor smiled at her. 'Good point. That means the answer is likely to be something a lot more interesting.'

'What was that noise?' Sid asked.

All three went quiet, trying to listen. There was a heavy thumping sound, and it seemed to be getting nearer and nearer.

'Do you have a marching band that might be getting in some late-night marching practice?' the Doctor whispered.

Sid shook his head.

They crept down the corridor and peered round the corner. Emma gasped in horror.

Four short, burly figures were trooping towards them. Each wore a dark blue uniform that seemed to be something between spacesuit and armour. There were large, rounded helmets on top. Two carried long, thin devices in their hands. The others held weapons that looked like compact machine guns. The Doctor knew that they were all deadly.

He flung himself back round the corner, pulling Emma and Sid with him. 'I said the answer was likely to be interesting,' he said. 'And that's what I call interesting.'

'But what are they?' asked Sid.

The Doctor took a deep breath. 'Sontarans!' he said.

Chapter Three

The Doctor waited until the Sontarans had gone past. Then he led Sid and Emma out from their hiding place.

'We've got to get people out of here,' he told the nervous pair. 'Sontarans are ruthless and deadly, and no one is safe if they're around.'

'But what are they?' asked Sid, his eyes wide.

The Doctor explained quietly as they crept away. 'They're warriors from the planet Sontar,' he said. 'They live only for battle, and it's almost impossible to defeat them in combat. They only have one weakness, a little hole in the back of the neck called a probic vent. If you hit one there, he'll fall over.'

'That sounds like good advice,' said Sid.

'It's not,' the Doctor said. 'Good advice is to keep as far away from them as possible.'

'But what are they doing here?' asked Emma.

The Doctor shrugged. 'The war must have moved over here. Every few hundred years it heads towards this solar system, and Earth becomes a key battle site.' He sighed. 'It's a war that will never end. The Sontarans have been fighting the Rutans for ever, or that's what it seems like.'

'The... Rutans?' said Emma.

'Big green shape-changing amphibious blobs.'

'Hold on a second,' said Sid. 'Amphibi-what?'

'They live both on land and in water. Like frogs. And they're deadly warriors. Not like frogs. Well, not like *most* frogs.' He paused for a second, thoughtful.

'The common room's just down here,' Sid said. 'Anyone who's not in bed yet will be in there. I warn you, though, they'll think this is a plot to rob them of a place in the Games. No one trusts anyone else round here.'

There were two young women and one man in the common room. Sid introduced Karl and Jess, both tall, good-looking and black, just like Sid. Karl was a sprinter and Jess was a long-jumper. The third person was a petite red-headed gymnast called Holly.

All three seemed on edge. The first thing they wanted to know was what had happened when the lights went out. They were expecting bad news – but not the news that the Doctor gave them.

12

They listened, frowning, while the Doctor explained about the Sontarans. He wasn't surprised to find they didn't believe him.

'It's a trick,' Jess said, just as Sid had predicted. 'You want us to leave BASE so we'll lose our chance to make the teams.'

'No,' said the Doctor calmly, 'I want you to leave BASE so you'll gain a chance to live. If you stay here, you are in great danger.'

'From these Sun-tanners?' she sneered, clearly not convinced by anything he'd said.

'Sontarans.' That was Emma. 'We saw them, Sid and me. I agree with the Doctor. We have to get out of here.'

'If I don't get a good night's sleep, I won't be able to run well in the morning,' Karl said. 'Is someone paying you to upset my training?'

The Doctor slapped his hand against his forehead. 'The only running you'll be doing is running away!' he told the young man. 'This is silly! Don't you trust anyone?'

Sid laughed grimly. 'You ain't seen nothing yet, Doctor. Notice that this lot all do different sports? You won't even get two teammates in the same room. They'd stab each other in the back before you could say "Paula Radcliffe".'

The Doctor shook his head, amazed. 'How did you ever manage to work together long enough to cover up three murders? That really was a triumph of selfishness over spite.'

Sid shrugged. He turned to the others. 'Look, it's not a trick, right. These monsters have got guns.'

In the end, Karl, Holly and even Jess agreed to go with the Doctor. 'But if there's no sign of these alien things, I'm coming straight back,' said Jess, grumpily.

The six of them made their way upstairs towards the bedrooms. 'I could set off the fire alarm,' said Holly. 'That would wake everyone up, and give them a reason to get out. Then you wouldn't have to explain all about the monsters.'

'Nah,' said Jess. 'Leave them there. If the monsters get them all, I get a place in the Games.'

The Doctor ignored Jess, but gave Holly a big smile. 'The fire alarm's a good idea. But there could be panic, people running here, there and all over the place. Then the Sontarans might get a bit trigger-happy, and we really don't want that.'

They were still trying to come up with a plan when they reached the upper floor. But it turned out that they didn't need one. They were too late.

'Are they the aliens?' gasped Jess, no longer stroppy. She stared as two Sontarans herded a crowd of sleepy, scared people down the corridor at gun-point.

'Oh yes,' said the Doctor. He took a deep breath and pointed away from the Sontarans. 'Right. You five, that way. Quick and quiet as you can. Use doors, windows, cat flaps, anything, just get out of here and don't come back.'

'But what about you?' asked Emma.

He shrugged. 'Someone's got to get the rest of the students out. That's my job.' She didn't look happy, so he kept on. 'I mean, that's my *job*. No pay, no sick days, no desk with my name on it, but it's what I do. Fight monsters. Rescue people.'

'I hear you, man,' said Karl. 'I'm out of here!' The tall sprinter hurried off, his trainers making no noise as he ran. Jess, Holly and Sid followed. With a last glance at the Doctor, Emma went too.

There was a door at the end of the corridor leading to a fire escape. Karl pushed down the metal bar that was supposed to open it. Nothing happened.

'It can't be locked!' Jess said, a note of fear in her voice. 'You're not allowed to lock fire exits! It's the law!' She rattled the metal bar as

Sid came forward to have a go. His arm muscles stood out as he pushed, but the door just would not open.

The Doctor had started to follow the Sontarans. He returned to the athletes when he heard the panic at the door. He pulled a slim metal tube from his pocket as he joined them.

'Sonic screwdriver,' he told the frantic five. 'Don't worry, this will get you out.'

He twisted the end of the sonic and the tip began to glow blue. He waved it across the fire door.

Nothing happened.

'Right,' said the Doctor. 'Everyone back downstairs.'

They hurried back the way they'd come, then Karl led the way to the building's main door. It wouldn't open, even with the sonic screwdriver.

'We've got to get out!' yelled Jess. The others tried to 'shhh' her, but she was too upset. She ran into the common room and picked up a chair.

'No!' cried Emma, realising what Jess planned to do. 'The Sontarans will hear the crash!'

It was too late. Jess raised the chair above her head and threw it as hard as she could at a window.

Everyone held their breath.

The chair bounced off the window.

The Doctor sighed. 'I'm sorry,' he said. 'It looks like the Sontarans have sealed the building.'

'You mean...?' Holly began.

Emma finished the sentence for her. 'We're trapped,' she said.

Chapter Four

Everyone was quiet for a few moments as this sank in. Then the Doctor gave a yelp. 'No, we're not trapped!' He led the way out of the common room. 'Now, I don't normally do this, and you've all got to promise not to touch anything. We're going to my ship.'

'Your ship?' Emma said. 'You mean, your spaceship?'

'Spaceship, time ship, whatever you want to call it.' A sad look crossed his face. 'I met some good people not long ago, and the Sontarans killed them. I don't want that to happen again, not if I can help it. I'm getting you out of here.'

They were halfway to the TARDIS when everything went dark.

Holly gasped. 'The power's gone off again!'

There was silence. The Doctor guessed that all the students were thinking the same thing. After a few moments, Sid put the thought into words. 'Every time there's been a power cut, someone's died.'

'Not every time,' said Emma. 'No one died earlier tonight when the power went off, did they?'

'Perhaps we just haven't found the body yet,' said Jess, her voice sounding scared. 'Perhaps it's floating in the swimming pool like Laura, or shoved under the stairs like Andy. Perhaps we'll go round the corner and trip over it!'

Holly stumbled and gave a shriek. 'The body!' she cried. 'It's the body!'

The Doctor whipped his torch from his pocket and turned it on. The light showed what Holly had fallen over. It wasn't a body. It was a pair of chunky rubber boots.

'I fell over these earlier!' the Doctor told them. 'That means we're right by the TARDIS!'

He waved the torch beam around, looking for his ship.

It lit up the helmeted head of a Sontaran, standing right in front of them. There was a large black gun in its hand that was pointing straight at the Doctor.

Then the Sontaran flung up its other hand to cover the eye slots in its helmet.

The Doctor yelled in delight. 'It's dazzled!' he cried. 'As long as I shine the torch in its eyes, it can't see us!'

He jumped to one side as the alien fired a shot

towards the voice. He didn't let the torch beam waver, though.

The Doctor thrust a hand in his pocket and pulled out the TARDIS key. He threw it back over his shoulder, yelling 'Catch!'

'Got it!' Jess called back.

'Good girl! Now, there's a big blue box just over there. You won't be able to see that it's blue in the dark, but trust me. Let everyone in and wait for me.'

A laser beam from the Sontaran's gun briefly lit up the TARDIS. 'There you go!' cried the Doctor as he hopped out of the way again.

He could hear the footsteps as Jess hurried forward. 'Where's the keyhole?' she called. 'Oh wait, here it—'

There was a huge flash. Pale green light flared around the TARDIS. Holly and Emma screamed, Sid and Karl yelled, but there was no sound from Jess.

They all blinked as the lights came back on. Then they saw Jess. She was lying on the floor by the TARDIS. A melted, twisted scrap of metal in her hand was all that remained of the key. Her eyes were open, but saw nothing. She was dead.

Chapter Five

There was no time to mourn Jess.

With the lights back on, the Sontaran was able to see again. Its gun was steady now, pointing straight at the Doctor.

'You will come with me!' the alien said, its voice deep and harsh.

'Ah,' said the Doctor. 'The thing is, you see, I don't really want to do that.'

'Then you will die.' The monster's massive, three-fingered hands gripped the weapon tighter.

'Ah!' said the Doctor again. 'I don't really want to do that either!'

He was staring straight at the Sontaran. He hoped that if he kept eye contact, the alien would forget about the students behind it. They were all frozen to the spot, none of them daring to move.

'And *you* might not want me to do that, if you knew who I was,' he continued. 'I'm not one of the sports students.'

Out of the corner of his eye he noticed the

toolbox, still lying by the TARDIS. 'Not saying I don't like sports, of course. Darts, now. Quite keen on darts. Just like little javelins, they are.'

He saw javelin-thrower Sid's head jerk up at that.

'Except that instead of trying to throw them a long way,' he went on, 'you're trying to hit a small target.'

'Stop your chatter!' shouted the Sontaran, still aiming the gun at the Doctor. 'If you do not belong to this place, you will tell me why you are here!'

'Well, I've come to fix things,' said the Doctor. 'Come to fix problems using my trusty toolbox. Everyone should have a toolbox. Full of handy tools. Chisels, screwdrivers – just like little darts...'

The Sontaran kept staring at the Doctor. Its gun was still pointing towards him. But then, very slowly, it toppled forward like a felled tree. A screwdriver was sticking out of the back of its neck.

'Ha ha!' The Doctor punched the air, and ran forward to shake Sid's hand. 'Well done you! You shouldn't be an athlete, you should be a spy, you're that good at working out coded messages!'

Sid looked a bit bashful. 'I should have thought

24

of it myself,' he said. 'You'd told us before about the Sontaran's weak spot, and the toolbox was just sitting there…'

'Is it dead?' asked Holly, looking down at the prone alien.

The Doctor shook his head. 'Just knocked out,' he said. 'So we'd better make tracks before it comes round.'

All five of them turned to the TARDIS.

'Jess is dead, though,' said Emma. She was staring at the girl who still lay in front of the ship's doors.

'Massive electric shock, just like the others,' said the Doctor, kneeling down beside the body. He looked at the melted key in Jess's hand and pulled a face.

'Can we get into your ship without the key?' asked Karl.

The Doctor wrinkled his nose. 'I can sort that. I'm more worried that the TARDIS is still packing a charge, though.'

'Surely Jess would have earthed it,' Karl said.

The Doctor was already pulling on the heavy rubber boots. He added a pair of thick insulated gloves that were poking out of the toolbox. 'Proper electrician's gear,' he commented. 'Better safe than sorry.'

He took a couple of steps towards the TARDIS,

a gloved hand outstretched. A bright green spark leapt from the ship, arcing through the air towards him.

The Doctor backed off. 'If I hadn't had these on,' he said, peeling off the rubber gloves one finger at a time, 'there would have been toasted Doctor on the menu.'

'So we can't get out in your ship,' said Sid.

The Doctor shook his head. 'No. We're stuck here with the Sontarans.'

Chapter Six

They hurried through the corridors. The four students had all decided to stay with the Doctor. None of them fancied trying to hide from the Sontarans on their own.

It was easy to track down the rest of the athletes. The Doctor and his friends just followed the sound of screams.

'They're in the gym hall,' Holly told the Doctor. She shivered. 'What are they doing in there?'

'That's what we've got to find out,' he replied.

Emma looked thoughtful. 'Doesn't the hall have a viewing gallery?' she said. 'They might not notice us if we were up there, but we could see what was going on.'

The Doctor beamed at her. 'Good plan!' he said. He spun around. 'Lead the way!'

They hurried up a flight of stairs and into the viewing gallery. There they crouched down, not wanting to be spotted by any Sontarans who looked their way. Bent almost double, they crept to the front of the gallery and peered into the gym.

Frantic, crying students filled one end of the hall. They were dressed in nightclothes. Some of them seemed dazed. Perhaps they didn't know that they were awake and thought they were still in a nightmare. At the other end, towering above them, was a Sontaran. The Doctor did a double take. Then he realised that the short alien was standing on a vaulting horse. 'I hope he falls off,' he muttered.

A Sontaran stood on either side of the horse. 'Silence!' shouted the Sontaran on the left.

The Sontaran on the other side echoed him. 'Silence! Silence!' Their guns swung from side to side, covering the panicking students.

A laser beam flew into the crowd. There were cries, but it didn't seem as though anyone had been hit. A warning shot. The students fell silent except for a few sobs.

'Silence for Major Stenx!' shouted the left-hand Sontaran.

'Silence for Stenx the Strong-hearted!' shouted the right-hand Sontaran, despite the fact that the students had clearly got the message already.

The central Sontaran carefully lifted up his helmet. Emma clapped a hand to her mouth.

There were gasps all around the gym as the alien's head was revealed. Its skin was the muddy brown of a rotten apple. Its head was as domed and hairless as the same fruit cut in half. Little piggy eyes squinted from either side of a large nose. A small black tongue flicked in and out of a slit of a mouth as the Sontaran spoke.

'I am Major Stenx of the Twelfth Sontaran Battle Fleet. This building is now under Sontaran control,' he announced. 'You there!' A three-fingered hand jabbed towards a scared-looking young man near the front of the crowd.

'That's Jimmy,' whispered Karl.

'What is the purpose of this place?' Stenx went on.

'This is... this is BASE,' the lad stammered. 'We're training for the Games.'

'Games?' echoed Stenx. 'What are these "Games" of which you speak?'

Jimmy could barely speak for fear. 'The... the Globe Games,' he said at last. 'We compete with other countries in sports.'

'Ah!' Stenx's thin mouth curved into a smile. 'You are warriors, then, of a sort. This is good! Sontarans, too, think training is vital if one is to defeat one's enemies. Perhaps you will provide a challenge for Sontaran soldiers, unlike the rest of your feeble species.'

Stenx ordered Jimmy to come forward. Trembling, the young man did so, and stood in front of the vaulting horse.

'Tell me,' said Stenx, 'in what sport do you compete?'

'I'm a hurdler,' Jimmy said. His voice was so low that the Doctor had to strain to hear.

'A hurdler?'

'I jump over hurdles. And run. Run and jump. Over hurdles.'

'Run and jump.' Stenx leaned over to speak to one of his aides. The Sontaran nodded, then stomped over to a balance beam and knelt down, appearing to inspect it. Stenx turned back to Jimmy. 'You could jump over that?' he asked, pointing at the beam.

Jimmy nodded.

'Good. Do so. I wish to see this "running and jumping".'

The Doctor stared down at the Sontarans. Every instinct he possessed was telling him to leap from the viewing gallery and confront them. He knew, though, that he had more chance of stopping them if they didn't know he was there. So far, at least, they hadn't harmed anyone.

Down in the gym, Jimmy had started to run towards the beam. As he picked up pace, the worry seemed to drain from his face. He was an athlete. This was what he did.

The youth soared gracefully into the air. He cleared the beam easily, and came in to land. His foot touched the floor.

There was an explosion. It happened in a split second, and no one had time to turn away. All the students saw exactly what happened to Jimmy.

The Doctor saw it too. His hands were on top of the barrier and his knees were bent. He was ready to vault down into the hall before the sound had even died away.

Strong arms dragged him back. To the Doctor's enormous surprise, Emma was pulling him down to the floor of the gallery. Her swimmer's muscles were straining to hold back the angry Time Lord. 'Don't!' she whispered. 'If they catch you, you'll condemn us all to death.'

'But that boy, Jimmy,' the Doctor began.

Emma shook her head. 'It's too late for him. You have to stay free, for the rest of us. You're our only hope.'

Down in the hall, Major Stenx was speaking to the shocked students. 'An interesting study. The youth had speed and some degree of skill, but his mind was not alert. He failed to detect the charge placed by Captain Skeed.' He sneered.

31

'I believe you humans have a saying which he did not observe: "Look before you leap". He did not, and so is no match for the might of the Sontarans!' Stenx thumped a fist against his palm. 'Sontar-ha!'

The two Sontarans beside him took up the cry. 'Sontar-ha! Sontar-ha!'

Up in the gallery, the Doctor was nearly boiling over with anger. He wanted to be down there, facing the Sontarans. It was only Emma's hand on his arm that was holding him back.

'I need to know why they're here!' he hissed through closed teeth. 'Then maybe I'll be able to stop them.'

Karl, Sid and Holly had crept closer, perhaps feeling safer near the Doctor. 'Maybe it's something to do with the swimming pool,' Sid suggested. 'That's where the first death happened.'

The Doctor nodded. 'As good a place to start as any,' he said. 'Let's go.'

As they crept from the gallery, the Sontarans' shouts echoed after them. 'Sontar-ha! Sontar-ha! SONTAR-HA!'

Chapter Seven

The Doctor and the four students made their way out of the viewing gallery. They headed towards the swimming pool.

'I don't think we're going to learn anything, though,' said Emma. 'I know Laura died there, but the other two didn't.'

Holly nodded. 'Well, yeah. But Andy's body was found quite near the pool area, and Joe was Laura's boyfriend – he might have been trying to find out what had happened to her.'

The Doctor's ears pricked up. This was news to him.

'You didn't tell me two of the victims were a couple,' he said to Emma. 'I thought no one round here spoke to anyone else!'

She wrinkled her nose. 'Sorry. I forgot you wouldn't have known.' She shook her head. 'But I still don't think the pool's important. We've been swimming there every day since and not seen anything odd.'

'Ah, but you didn't know what you were looking for!' he said.

Karl looked hopeful. 'And you do?' he said eagerly.

'Well, no,' said the Doctor, and the students sighed. 'But I am an ace private eye with a degree in detecting and a licence to sleuth. I'll work it out.'

They reached the pool room. The Doctor asked Karl to stay on guard, watching for Sontarans. The sprinter seemed relieved not to have to come inside with the others.

The Doctor flicked a switch as they entered, and the pool area was flooded with harsh white light. Out of the corner of his eye he saw Emma shiver.

'Cold?' he said.

She shook her head and pointed at the pool. 'That's where she was,' she said. 'Laura. You could just see her hair, floating out on the surface like seaweed.'

The Doctor patted her shoulder awkwardly. 'Don't worry. I'm not going to let anything like that happen again.' He paused for a second, trying to think of something else to say. 'You know, it is a bit chilly in here. Indoor pools are usually toasty warm.'

'The heating went out with the first power cut,' said Emma, still staring at the water.

'Ah.' There didn't seem to be a lot else to say.

The Doctor was itching to begin his search. He started to roam around the room, looking for anything that seemed out of place. Notices on the walls warned about the dangers of running on the wet tiles. The Doctor was still wearing the rubber boots, though, and he was as sure-footed as a cat.

After a few minutes, Sid called over, 'Is it just me, or can anyone else smell something?'

They all sniffed. 'It's just chlorine,' said Emma. 'They put loads of it in the pool to keep it clean. You'd get used to it if you were down here all the time.'

Sid shook his head. 'No, there's something else.'

The Doctor joined Sid. He shut his eyes, letting his keen Time Lord sense of smell take over. 'You're right, there is something,' he said, and began to sniff like a bloodhound, with his eyes still closed. Only Sid's quick reactions stopped the Doctor walking straight into the swimming pool.

After a short detour, he was back on the trail again. 'It's over here,' he said at last, opening his eyes. He was standing by a grille in the floor. He peered through it, but couldn't see anything.

After a few waves of the sonic screwdriver, the Doctor was able to pull up the grating. Using his torch, he examined the opening, and finally reached an arm down the hole.

Emma, Sid and Holly watched with bated breath as the Doctor pulled his arm out again. His hand came into view. It was holding on to another hand, gripping it as if pulling someone up through the floor.

But there was no person on the other end of the hand. There wasn't even an arm.

Holly turned round and was sick. Sid and Emma looked as though they were thinking of joining her.

The Doctor laid the hand on the tiled floor. 'Someone's tipped about a gallon of chlorine over it. They probably hoped to hide the rotting smell. That makes it harder to judge how long it's been down there, but I'd say about a week.'

'But that's before Laura died!' said Sid.

'Oh yes.' The Doctor nodded. 'And none of the bodies you showed me had a hand missing. There weren't just those three deaths. There were four.' He turned and stared at the students. 'At least.'

Emma opened her mouth, but the Doctor never heard what she had to say. An alarm blared out, making them all jump. Then a hoarse Sontaran voice boomed out of a speaker. 'Alert! Alert! Humans are still loose in the building!

They must be found!'

'What's happening?' cried Holly.

'Well,' said the Doctor, 'I reckon the Sontaran that Sid knocked out has just woken up. The building is sealed, so they know we must still be around somewhere.'

'We've got to get out of here!' Emma called, running towards the door. She flung it open, but was met by Karl, coming the other way.

'Sontarans!' he yelled. 'They're nearly here!'

The five looked around in dismay. There was only one other exit, a tunnel leading to the changing rooms. They dashed towards it.

Halfway across the floor, Holly slipped on the wet tiles and landed on her back. Unable to stop in time, Sid fell over the prone gymnast. Karl held out a hand, but Sid yelled in pain as he tried to get up. He fell back, clutching his ankle. Emma tried to help Holly, but she just lay there, muttering about being dizzy.

Heavy footsteps were getting nearer and nearer. A Sontaran shadow fell across the doorway. There was no time now to get to the tunnel, even if Sid and Holly could walk.

Quick as a flash, Emma jumped into the pool, her dive barely creating a single ripple. The Doctor hardly had a second to reflect on her skill, before two helmeted Sontarans entered.

He recognised Captain Skeed by the military symbols on his collar, and assumed the other Sontaran must be the one they'd met by the TARDIS. Both held weapons.

'Ah!' cried Skeed. 'Here they are. Did you think you could escape the Sontarans for long?'

'Not really,' said the Doctor, joining them. 'Oh well. We'd better get going, then.' He began to walk out of the door.

'Not so fast, human!' Skeed put up a hand to stop him. 'Our great leader Stenx has said you must be punished for your conduct. You are to take part in the first ever Sontaran Games!'

'Really?' said the Doctor. 'Lucky old me! Well, I don't want to miss that.' He started walking again.

Skeed raised his weapon, pointing it at the three students. 'These others will also take part in the Games.'

The Doctor waved a hand. 'What, them? They wouldn't be much good. One's got a busted ankle and one's just whacked her head on the floor.' He waggled a finger round his ear. 'Can't think straight. No use at all.'

'We will find a use for them,' said the second Sontaran, starting towards the little group.

'No, no, all right, they're coming,' said the Doctor hurriedly, as Holly and Sid limped

38

towards the door, helped by Karl. He didn't want the Sontarans getting any closer to the pool. If Emma could remain free, they might still have a chance. But how much longer could she stay under the water? If they didn't get out of here soon, she would have to come up for air and all would be lost.

The Doctor gave a sigh of relief as the three students finally made it across the floor, and he started hustling them out through the door. 'Come on, come on, we don't want to keep the Sontarans waiting. It's the first ever Sontaran Games, you know.'

He risked a quick glance back. Was that a dark shape at the bottom of the pool? With a sigh, the Doctor turned away as Skeed slammed the door. Emma had been under the water for almost three minutes – could she possibly have held her breath for that long?

The Doctor, Karl, Sid and Holly were led back to the gym hall. Holly seemed dazed still, and was holding on to the Doctor's arm. Sid leant on Karl, and was wincing in pain with every step.

Skeed seemed interested in the students, and asked the Doctor about them. 'The damaged one, what is his sport?' the Sontaran said.

The Doctor glanced back at Sid, unsure if

telling the truth would get the lad into trouble. 'Oh, throwing things mainly,' he said lightly.

Skeed nodded. 'Ah. Then he is of little use to us. All missiles have been removed. Is that not right, Lieutenant Slorr?'

The other Sontaran stood up straight. 'Following my disgrace, I offered Major Stenx my weapon!' he said hotly. 'He refused to accept it, as all are needed to find—'

'Silence!' Captain Skeed's eyes burned through the slots in his helmet as he shouted. 'Do not add to your folly by speaking of Sontaran concerns in front of these humans!'

The Doctor smiled to himself. Dissent in the ranks was always good. Besides, he now knew something he hadn't known before. The Sontarans were searching for something. The question was – what?

Chapter Eight

The gym had changed since the Doctor had last been in it. For a start, all the students had gone. Only the sad, huddled body of Jimmy, the Sontarans' victim, was left.

A number of pieces of sporting equipment had been dragged onto the floor. Stenx was walking around the room, inspecting them.

The Sontaran major turned as the Doctor and his friends were brought in. He strode over and looked the four up and down.

Holly flinched as he reached out and touched her throat. 'A female,' Stenx said. 'Females possess less speed and strength than the males. They are inferior.'

Holly let go of the Doctor's arm and faced Stenx. 'Oh no we aren't,' she said, as she walked forward and fell over.

Stenx sneered. 'Point proved.'

'She's one of the best gymnasts in the country!' Karl put in. 'Maybe *the* best. She's not inferior to anyone.'

The Doctor smiled at Karl as he helped Holly

to her feet. He hadn't imagined it – the students were starting to be nicer to each other.

'She's hurt,' the Doctor told Stenx. 'She may be concussed. She needs help.'

'To help a damaged human would be a waste of Sontaran resources,' said the major.

'Two of them are damaged,' put in Captain Skeed. He pointed at Karl and the Doctor. 'Only these two are fit for our purpose.'

Stenx moved over to Karl and lifted his chin with one stubby finger. 'What skill do you possess, human?'

'I'm a runner,' gasped Karl. 'A sprinter.'

The Sontaran gave a nod. Without a neck, the whole of his upper body moved forward as he did so. 'Speed is good, but not vital,' he said. 'Yes, we will use this one first. It will not matter if he dies.'

Lieutenant Slorr grabbed Karl's arm and began to drag him forward. The scared youth gave the Doctor a pleading look.

The Doctor coughed. 'You haven't asked me what skill I possess,' he said quietly.

Stenx turned towards him. 'Well, human?'

'Quite well, thank you. But not human.'

Four guns pointed at him instantly. 'This is the one!' shouted Skeed. 'The one we have been searching for! Cover him, Lieutenant Skezz!' The fourth Sontaran pointed his gun at the Doctor.

The Doctor frowned. He had wanted to distract them. He hadn't dreamed he would turn out to be the prey they were hunting.

But no. If they had been looking for him, surely they would have recognised the TARDIS.

'Do you deny you are the shape-shifter?' yelled Skezz.

'Yes, I deny it!' said the Doctor. Then he thought for a second. 'Well, maybe *a* shape-shifter. I don't do it on a daily basis, though, just, oooh, maybe once a century. Does that count?' He grinned. 'But I know who you're looking for, now, Major Stinks.'

'The name is Stenx!' yelled Captain Skeed. 'Stenx the Strong-hearted!'

'That's what I said,' agreed the Doctor. 'Stinks the Strong-f—' He broke off, as Skeed's gun swung round to point at Karl.

'You will show respect to the major,' Skeed growled. 'If you do not, I will kill this human as an example to you.'

Every trace of a smile vanished from the Doctor's face. 'Oh, I wouldn't do that,' he said, and his stare made even the Sontarans flinch. He lowered his voice. 'You never did ask me what my skill was. Bit rude to assume I've just got the one, by the way. I've got lots.'

43

Stenx waved his gun, but the Doctor would not be cowed and kept on. 'But the main one, the big one, is the skill to know about everything. Well, almost everything. More or less everything. Perhaps a bit more less than more. Still, I know lots and lots about you. The Sontarans. In fact, one of my other skills is defeating you. Want to hang around while I do it again, or will you leave this planet now?'

'How dare you speak to Major Stenx like that!' shouted Captain Skeed. 'Who do you think you are, creature who is not human?'

The Doctor smiled. 'I'm a Time Lord,' he said. 'I hope that answers all your questions.'

For a moment, none of the Sontarans spoke. Then Stenx smiled. 'The ancient enemy,' he said. 'What a prize to bring Sontaran High Command!' He turned to his fellow Sontarans. 'Comrades! When we arrived on this planet, we thought merely of gaining a single kill. Then the trail led here, and we gained the chance to collect data on humans. Now we can also assess the weak points of a Time Lord! For the glory of Sontar!'

The others echoed his cry. 'For the glory of Sontar!'

The Doctor was tempted to remind them that he was the last of the Time Lords. Anything they learned from him wouldn't be of much use to them in the future. But then they might decide to just kill him straight away, so he kept quiet.

The Doctor was locked up in a cupboard. Empty racks were labelled 'javelins', 'bows' and so on. The Sontarans had removed anything that might be used as a weapon against them. He tried to open the door with his sonic screwdriver, but failed.

There was one glimmer of hope, though.

The Doctor had been led under the edge of the viewing gallery. For a moment he'd thought it was raining indoors, as a spot of water hit his head. It wasn't rain, of course. He'd lifted his hand, wiped the wet spot and held his fingers to his nose. Was that the faintest whiff of chlorine? Could it be a drip of water from a soaking wet swimmer, hiding somewhere above him?

He'd raised his head, slowly, hoping the Sontarans wouldn't spot what he was doing. He'd looked up at the gallery.

A hand had crept over the edge, and given him a thumbs-up.

The Doctor had smiled. If Emma was there, he still had a chance.

Chapter Nine

Now the Doctor could hear comings and goings from the gym hall. Sontarans stamped past. There were sounds of heavy equipment being dragged across the floor. Lighter footsteps followed, and cries that told him students were being led through the hall.

Then after what seemed like a very long wait, there came the sound he was hoping for. A faint knock on the cupboard door.

'Hello?' he whispered.

'Doctor?' a voice whispered back. It was Emma!

'Can you let me out of here?' the Doctor asked.

'No, it's been deadlocked,' she told him.

He sighed. 'Well, what's going on?'

'Not sure. The Sontarans are taking all the students into the arena.'

'The arena?' The Doctor imagined the sort of place where the Romans threw people to the lions.

He told Emma that, and she laughed. 'More

the sort of place where they hold sports events and sometimes pop concerts,' she said.

'Do you know if Karl's OK?' the Doctor asked. The last he'd seen of the sprinter was Lieutenant Slorr leading him towards a door. Where the door went, he didn't know.

'They took him to the arena too.' To the Doctor's surprise, Emma's voice sounded more cross than upset.

'What's up?' he asked. 'Don't be angry with Karl. I thought you lot were getting past all that blaming and snapping at each other. It wasn't his fault we were captured.'

For a few seconds she was quiet, and the Doctor wondered if she'd left. Then she spoke. 'I'm not cross with Karl. I'm cross with you!'

The Doctor blinked. He hadn't been expecting that.

'Why?'

'You had to go and tell them you were a Time Lord, didn't you?'

'I had to distract them!' the Doctor said. 'Karl was in danger.'

'So what? You had a chance of helping us all if you'd just kept a low profile.'

The Doctor remembered Emma's hand holding him back in the gallery. He'd wanted to jump down then, and she'd stopped him.

'I can't do that,' he said. 'Let one person die, in case someone more important comes along that I have to save? How could you ever make that choice? I wouldn't be me if I did that.'

'But it's selfish,' Emma told him. 'Whole worlds might be destroyed, because you had to save one person.'

The Doctor laughed. 'One day Karl might save the world,' he said. 'Then we'd be in a pretty pickle, if I'd let the Sontarans kill him.'

'You haven't stopped them, though,' Emma told him. 'You've just risked both your necks.'

The Doctor hated every word that she'd said. He disagreed with every comment she'd made. But he was forced to admit she might have a point there.

He took a deep breath. 'All I can do is my best,' he said.

Suddenly, there came the *thump-thump-thump* of heavy Sontaran boots.

The Doctor held his breath. He didn't like Emma's point of view, but he didn't want her captured. She was his sole trump card, the only thing the Sontarans didn't know about.

He heard a couple of Sontarans call out to each other. They seemed to be checking that the Doctor was still locked up.

There were no hiding places in the hall. The

Doctor couldn't see how Emma could possibly get away in time.

If she was caught – they were all doomed.

Chapter Ten

The Doctor listened hard. There was no scream from Emma, no Sontaran cry of triumph as she was spotted.

The Doctor let out his breath again.

Then came the sound of the bolts being drawn back, and the cupboard door was opened. Lieutenant Slorr stood in the doorway. He beckoned to the Doctor.

'Who, me?' the Doctor said, checking over his shoulder. There was no one else there, so he walked forward to join the lieutenant. He took a quick look around, but there was no sign of Emma. How she'd escaped he didn't know.

Slorr stared at the Doctor through the slits in his helmet. 'Our fearless leader Stenx has bestowed a great honour on you.'

The Doctor stared back. 'I wouldn't call being locked in a cupboard that much of an honour. Tell you what, if you think it's so great, why don't you try it? I'd be happy to turn the key.'

'That is not the honour! You are to be the first to take part in the first ever Sontaran Games!

You will die gloriously for the Sontaran cause.'

'Don't count on it,' said the Doctor under his breath.

Slorr led the Doctor to a door on the far side of the gym. It was the same one Karl had been heading towards earlier.

Through the door was a covered walkway. The Doctor tried to see where they were going, but it was pitch black ahead.

He felt a breeze on his face, and realised they were now outside. Even though it was the middle of the night, the summer air was warm.

Slorr stopped prodding him forward. The Doctor was tempted to make a break for it, but Stenx's earlier words came back to him. 'Look before you leap.' If he ran, he might be playing into the Sontarans' hands. If only he could see where he was!

His wish was granted. Suddenly, the whole area was lit up.

The Doctor was standing in the centre of a sports arena. There were tiers of seats all around. Scared-looking students huddled on plastic chairs, but they barely filled up a couple of rows. The Doctor felt a bit cross. He was about to die gloriously for the Sontaran cause. They could at least have got in a good crowd.

He looked closely. Karl was there, right at the front. He looked unhurt. Sid was further back. Holly was at the end of a row. The Doctor was relieved to see them all. He was also pleased that there was no sign of Emma. She must still be free, and hiding.

Floodlights stood at the back of the seating, throwing harsh white light into the field. The Doctor squinted upwards. High above him, the air was shimmering. The Sontarans had put a force dome over the entire arena. That would make escape a lot harder.

There was something else above him, too. The Doctor stared. It looked like a giant hedgehog, rolled into a ball with all its prickles sticking out. Then he worked out what it was. It was all the sports gear that the Sontarans had taken away. All the javelins, poles, bows and arrows, shots and medicine balls, discuses and hammers. Anything that could be thrown at the Sontarans now floated up high in a force-sphere.

The Doctor thought his sonic screwdriver would be able to break through the force field. The trouble was, he wouldn't be able to reach it without flying. The Doctor was good at many, many things, but flying was not one of them.

He realised that he was now alone. Slorr had left him and was walking back to the edge of the arena. The three other Sontarans were spaced out around the edge of the field. What was he supposed to do now?

He didn't have to wait long to find out.

Stenx's voice echoed around the arena. 'Time Lord, you are honoured. You are the first to compete in the Sontaran Games. Survive, and you will be given a greater honour. You will face the mighty Sontarans in combat.'

'I'd prefer a medal,' called the Doctor. 'Or even a bunch of flowers.'

Stenx ignored him. 'The first game is the one hundred metres sprint,' he said. 'The one who loses will be put to death. The track will become lethal after fifteen Earth seconds. Let the Games begin!'

The Doctor was puzzled. There was the track before him. Even with heavy boots on, he could easily run it in less than fifteen seconds. But how could he win or lose?

The answer soon arrived, and he didn't like it. Captain Skeed was herding five students towards him at gunpoint. Karl was one of them.

The Doctor wasn't a trained athlete, but he wasn't human either. He knew he could probably outrun the others if he had to. Except if he did that, one of them would die.

The students were lining up at the start.

He couldn't let any of them die, which meant he had to lose. But if the Sontarans killed him, then the students didn't have much hope anyway. He thought back to what Emma had said to him, while he was locked in the cupboard. Let one person die, so you have the chance to save a lot more.

Skeed was raising his gun.

Perhaps he couldn't argue with Emma's logic. But he was the Doctor, and he was never going to let that happen. He'd just have to find another way.

The trouble was, all the athletes were now up on the starting blocks. They would be fast. Once the race started he'd only have about ten seconds to think of something.

'Go!' A streak of red laser fire shot out above their heads. The Doctor found himself running, almost without thinking about it. The students had hared off, wanting to save their own skins.

The Doctor stayed just behind them. The watching faces flashed past so quickly. He had seconds left to think of a plan. They were approaching the finish line.

Then he noticed that, all of a sudden, there were only four athletes in front of him.

Karl had dropped back.

The Doctor turned his head.

'We need you, Doctor!' Karl called. 'I won't let you lose!'

The Doctor's foot was almost at the line. He was going too fast, he couldn't stop. And there were only two seconds to go...

He changed direction in mid-air, spinning around and grabbing Karl's arm. His speed carried them both over the line and they landed in a heap. As they fell, a wall of energy shot up around the track. They lay there panting, and watched as orange gas filled the course they'd just taken.

Legs in dark blue armour came into view. The Doctor looked up to see that Stenx had joined them. Lieutenant Slorr was taking the four other students back to their seats.

'So,' said Stenx. 'You ran the race in exactly the same time. You are both losers. You will both be put to death.'

'Or both winners,' panted the Doctor. 'Major, you said, "The one who loses will be put to death." *The one*. But there was no one person who lost. You can't go back on your word. It wouldn't be honourable.'

The Doctor knew he was on shaky ground. Sontarans held honour above everything, but they did not always accept that it applied to other races too.

He was lucky. Stenx gave one of his whole-body nods, and Slorr hurried forward to remove Karl.

'Thank you,' the Doctor mouthed as the sprinter was led away. Karl had been willing to die so the Doctor could live. There was no question that the youth was a hero.

They'd both been lucky, though. The Sontarans wouldn't let the Doctor get away with the same trick twice.

His troubles were just beginning.

Chapter Eleven

The Doctor got to his feet. 'Do I get my medal now?' he asked Stenx.

The Sontaran sneered at him. 'There are many races to come, Doctor. But I thank you for the data you have provided. We now know the speed that humans and Time Lords can reach. We can make use of fast creatures. A running target may draw the enemy's fire, for example.'

The Doctor said nothing, but he was fuming inside.

'Now for the long jump!' called Stenx. 'It will be useful to find out how far humans can jump. Oh, and Time Lords too.' His thin mouth curved up in a cruel smile. 'Lieutenant Skezz, bring the humans.'

Skezz nodded to the major and moved over to the stands. Captain Skeed pushed the Doctor towards a sandy area. The long jump pit.

Soon, the Doctor was lined up behind five students. He hadn't met any of them before. That didn't mean he was willing to see harm come to them, though.

A line had been drawn across the pit, about six metres along. 'You will cross this line,' Stenx told them, pointing to it.

The first jumper, a tall, blonde-haired girl, seemed very scared. She stumbled as she began her run, but soon picked up speed. She reached the board, took one long stride then another, and sailed through the air. Her heels came down just over the line, and she began to sob with relief. For a few moments she just lay on the ground, shaking with sobs. In the end, Skezz forced her out of the pit at gunpoint.

The second athlete seemed less nervous. He gave the others a look that said 'you might be in trouble, but I'm not'. He started his run-up, pounding along as fast as any of the sprinters. He took one huge stride. He took a second, bringing his left leg forward, ready for the jump.

Something went wrong. His feet seemed to get tangled up, crossing over each other. He still jumped, but it was clear that he'd never reach the line.

He thudded into the sand, only a few metres along the pit.

For a second, he just looked cross with himself. Then something changed.

He began to scream.

The Doctor tried to run to him, but Lieutenant Skezz grabbed his arms.

Things were coming out of the sand. They were tiny, black and furry, and they had very pointed teeth. Soon they were swarming over the pit, all the way from the board to the line.

They were all over the failed athlete. But in less than a minute, there was no athlete left at all.

'Sontar Sand Shrews,' Skezz told the Doctor. 'Food is scarce in the deserts of Sontar, so they eat anything.'

The Doctor couldn't bring himself to speak. He could still hear the young man's screams in his head. Although now there were other screams too, from the watching crowd.

The next long-jumper in line, a young woman, was crying. 'I won't do it!' she sobbed. 'I won't, I won't!'

'You will jump,' Stenx told her.

'No, no, no,' she said.

'You can't expect them to jump, not after seeing that!' the Doctor cried.

'I can,' said Stenx. 'Because if they don't, this is what will happen to them.' Before the Doctor could react, Stenx had raised his wand-like gun. Red light spurted out of the end, and the crying girl fell to the floor.

The Doctor rushed to her, but it was too late. He stood up. All four Sontaran guns were pointing at him.

He couldn't think of a way out.

'We have to jump,' he told the other two. 'That way, we have a chance. If we don't jump, we have no chance at all.'

'But—' began a scared-looking youth.

The Doctor shook his head. 'No buts. You can all do this. You wanted to go to the Globe Games! Imagine the pressure there! World records at stake. TV cameras all over the place. Your family and friends watching. This should be a piece of cake compared to that!'

He was relieved to see them almost smile.

'That's it,' he said. 'You can do it.'

He was right. The two of them both made it over the line.

The Doctor gave a sigh of relief. His joy didn't last long, though. It was now his turn.

A blast from Skeed's gun shot over the Doctor's head, and he began to run. He knew he had to build up as much speed as he could. Nearly there. One huge stride, then another. His toe almost touched the fault line as he bent lower, preparing to jump.

He jumped... and soared away. He brought his back leg forward, bending so he was almost sitting in mid-air. It felt as if he spent hours above the ground, days, not mere seconds. Then he could feel himself slowing, getting lower. He was nearly at the line. He was going to make it!

Down, down, down...

His heels thudded into the sand – just before the line. Sand Shrews exploded out of the pit, snapping fiercely. They lunged at his feet...

Chapter Twelve

The Sand Shrews fell away, their teeth bouncing off the Doctor's heavy boots.

The Doctor almost felt sorry for them, as he jumped across the line, out of their reach.

The students were cheering from the stands. The Doctor felt like cheering himself. A few laser beams flying over the crowd soon shut them up, though. That made the Doctor serious again. He wondered what warped event he would have to face next.

Lieutenant Slorr had gone back inside the gym. Now he came out again, carrying a long, thick rope coiled over his arm. Skezz led forward seven students, all stocky and muscular. The Doctor felt very skinny as he was pushed into the middle of them. The eight of them were made to take hold of one end of the cord. 'If you let go of the rope, you will be killed,' the lieutenant told them.

'Tug of war,' the Doctor said. 'But who are we tugging against?' He knew that the Sontarans came from a world with much higher gravity than Earth. They had devices in their suits to help them adapt to the gravity of whatever planet they were on. Even so, the huge muscles they built up on their home world would help them win through.

The Doctor really hoped they weren't facing the Sontarans.

They weren't. They were facing something worse.

The Doctor looked on in shock as a huge robot came towards them. It stood high on bent metal legs. Black eyes on stalks snaked out of a wide head, perched on a blocky body. As they watched, eight metal cords sprung out of its sides, like long, thin arms.

These feelers weaved their way forward, then grasped the rope. First a left feeler, then a right feeler, all along the other end of the cord.

Beneath the centre of the rope was a red line. The Doctor dreaded to think what would happen to anyone who crossed it.

'Right,' he said to his team. 'You all know how a tug of war is played. You've all seen what happens to people who lose a Sontaran game. So we are going to pull and pull and pull, and we are going to win.'

There were murmurs of 'yeah' around the team.

'I can't hear you!' called the Doctor. 'We're going to win!'

'Yeah!' they cried.

There wasn't time for a longer pep talk. Skeed gave the signal, and the tug of war began.

It went well at first. Slowly but surely, the Doctor's team were forcing the robot towards the red line. Closer and closer it came. Almost there…

… and then the Doctor felt himself yanked forward so quickly he was barely able to keep upright.

The robot had been playing with them, judging their strength. Now they were running forward, unable to stop. The first athlete reached the red line almost before they knew what was happening.

With a *crackle*, a wall of energy sprang from the line. The girl barely had time to scream before it hit. When the last of the blue flashes died away, there was nothing on the ground but dust.

'Don't let go of the rope!' yelled the Doctor, as the others stood there, stunned. 'Keep pulling!'

He knew now that they didn't stand a chance. He wouldn't let them give up, though.

'It's too strong!' sobbed the young woman behind him.

'Yes, it is,' said the Doctor.

But something wasn't quite right. The robot was strong – but not as strong as he had expected. 'It's feeling Earth's gravity!' he cried. 'It must have controls to adjust its apparent mass, like the Sontarans' suits. If they were set for Sontar, it would seem even stronger!'

He peered hard – yes, there was a dial near the robot's head. The controls!

'If we could only get close enough, I could change things,' the Doctor told the athletes. 'I could make it feel really light, so we could pull it over the line easily.'

'But we can't get that close!' shouted a youth, as they were dragged towards the line again.

'I know!' cried the Doctor. 'What we need—' He broke off.

He couldn't believe his eyes. He'd have rubbed them, if he'd been able to let go of the rope. Surely he was dreaming?

Crawling across the arena, towards the robot, was Emma.

Two of the Sontarans were watching the crowd. The other two had their guns pointing at the Doctor's team. None of them were looking towards the robot. He had to make sure it stayed that way.

'Tell you what, let's sing a song!' he called.

'What? Are you joking?' shouted a young man from somewhere behind the Doctor.

'Not at all! A song to keep us all pulling as one. Just like the work songs from old America. The slaves would sing as they worked, to keep a rhythm. Maybe even to pass coded messages under the noses of their slavers. Come on! I'll sing the verses, you join in with the chorus! You'll all know this one!'

He began to sing at the top of his voice:

Swing low, sweet chariot,
Coming for to carry me home.

The rest of the team slowly took up the chorus:

Swing low, sweet chariot,
Coming for to carry me home.

The Doctor began to belt out a verse:

I looked at the robot and what did I see,
Coming for to carry me home.
A dial by its head that turned down should be,
Coming for to carry me home.

He glanced at the Sontarans. They didn't seem to have picked up on his message to Emma. She gave him a wave and started to climb up the robot's leg. He joined the team in belting out the chorus again, then added another verse. He hoped Emma was listening closely.

When the dial goes down,

> *the weight goes down too,*
> *Coming for to carry me home.*
> *Then jump off*
> *or the line will frazzle you,*
> *Coming for to carry me home.*

Emma was on the robot's shoulder as they sang the chorus again.

The Doctor kept singing to his team:

> *When that's done everyone must pull together,*
> *Coming for to carry me home.*
> *It'll feel to us even lighter than a feather,*
> *Coming for to carry me home.*

He saw Emma's hand reach out and grab the dial just below the robot's head.

She turned it.

The Doctor's team didn't pause. They just kept pulling.

'Stop!' he cried, but it was too late. For a moment, he thought the robot was flying. It came towards them like a bullet out of a gun.

The robot flew over the line. Energy beams leapt up from the ground. There was a crackling sound, then a huge explosion of blue and green. When it cleared, the robot was gone.

There was no sign of Emma.

The Doctor turned to his team, who were all crying with joy. 'The girl who was up there,' he said. 'Where did she go?'

'I didn't see her jump down,' said one, and the others all shook their heads.

'I don't think she had time,' said another. 'I think she was still on the robot when it came across the line. Oh no!'

'You should have let her get off before you started pulling,' said the Doctor. But he said it very quietly. He knew he hadn't been clear enough. Hard to let people know what to do in a song. It wasn't the team's fault.

His hearts sank. No human could have survived that flash of energy. If Emma hadn't got off the robot in time, she would have been fried.

Chapter Thirteen

'Doctor, look!' called Holly's voice from the stands.

A red laser beam flew over the Doctor's head, and he turned.

Holly hadn't been shouting a warning, though. She'd been trying to tell the Doctor about something else.

All four of the Sontarans were floating off the ground. They were trying to aim their guns, but couldn't manage it. Every few seconds they came back down to earth, but each step forward pushed them up again.

The Doctor gave a huge laugh. 'All their gravity controls must be connected to a central matrix! When Emma changed the robot's mass, the controls in the Sontarans' suits were affected too!' He shook his head, still grinning. 'Well, that's a clone race for you. What's good enough for one...'

Then he stopped smiling. There was no time to waste. This was the chance he'd been waiting for.

He ran to the tunnel that led to the gym. OK, so the building was sealed, but at least they'd be out of the way of the Sontarans.

This door was now locked too. Sealed by the Sontarans.

Back in the arena, he looked around, searching for clues. If only they could disable the Sontarans. But if anyone went near them, the Sontarans did their best to shoot. How long would it be before one hit its mark? Getting close enough to hit a Sontaran's weak spot, its probic vent, wasn't possible.

The Doctor looked upwards. The bundle of missiles was still hanging beneath the force dome.

The weapons were held in a force-sphere. Spheres often had a weak spot at the join. The Doctor stared. Yes, there it was. He could see a flicker of energy, a little white hole buzzing near the top. If he could get to it with his sonic screwdriver, he could release the missiles.

He glanced around the arena. Surely he could come up with a plan using a load of top athletes and a long rope... Yes!

'Tug of war team, to me!' he called.

The six strong young people ran over to the Doctor. 'Three this side, three that side,' he told them. 'Stretch the rope across, then climb up the stands as high as you can. Hold the rope tight.'

They didn't even ask why. They just nodded and ran off to do as he asked.

'Holly!' called the Doctor.

She jogged over to him.

'How are you feeling? Head OK?'

'I'm fine,' she said. 'What do you want me to do?'

'Well, I'm led to believe you might be the best gymnast in the country.' He pointed to the rope, now stretching across the arena at a height of several metres. It passed below the force-sphere containing the weapons. 'Could you get from that rope to that sphere?'

She nodded. 'With a little bit of help. Piece of cake!'

'The energy won't hurt you,' he told her. 'It's just holding everything in one place.' He took out his sonic screwdriver, and adjusted the settings. 'Just push it through that little white hole. I've set it for a 10-second delay. That should allow you to get off safely before the sphere vanishes. Do you think you can do that?'

'No problem,' she said. 'I can leap off and catch the rope as I go. Then I'll just shin along it. Plenty of time.'

The Doctor smiled at her, and then turned to the crowd.

'Keep as far back as possible,' he called. 'When that force-sphere goes, all the javelins, hammers, shots and things will fall to the ground. You don't want to be below when that happens.'

The students moved back. Holly called over five other gymnasts. Then they all climbed up the stand to where half the tug of war team waited.

The gymnasts pulled themselves along the rope until they were under the force-sphere. Three of them stood up. Two more climbed onto their shoulders.

There were gasps from the students watching below. No one had ever seen a feat like this before. A few let out yells of concern as Holly reached the top of the pyramid. Then she bent her knees – and leapt.

There were more cries from the crowd, but Holly made it. She grabbed a sticking-out javelin with both hands. Then she let go with one hand, and reached up for a pole. Slowly, she made her way towards the top of the force-sphere, and its weak spot.

The other gymnasts were making their way back down. They wanted to be out of the way when the missiles started to fall. This meant they were the only people looking into the arena, not up at Holly.

'Doctor!' called one of the gymnasts. The Doctor turned his head, and she pointed towards the Sontarans.

They were still floating along, but their steps weren't taking them so far off the ground. They were able to bring their arms down lower. They were also heading towards the Doctor, as best as they could.

'Their suits' gravity is going back to normal,' the Doctor said to himself. Any moment now, they could regain control of their guns. Then the Doctor and his friends were all doomed.

He glanced up at Holly. If only they had those missiles, things would be all right. 'Just put the screwdriver through that hole, Holly,' he called.

But something wasn't right. Holly had stopped moving.

'Are you all right?' asked the Doctor.

'I'm so dizzy!' she cried.

She raised a hand to her head. To the Doctor's horror, he saw the sonic screwdriver slip from her fingers. It fell down, down to the ground below.

It landed at the feet of Lieutenant Skezz.

Chapter Fourteen

'No!' shouted the Doctor. Without the screwdriver, they had no hope at all.

Skezz leant over to pick it up.

The Sontaran's arms went down, and his legs went up. Skezz hung in the air, turning lazy circles, unable to get himself back down. But he was still grabbing at the sonic screwdriver, every time his arms came near the ground. Now the other Sontarans were heading that way too.

There was a gasp from the watching students. Karl, the sprinter, had dashed out from the crowd. He darted past Skezz, and scooped up the sonic screwdriver.

The students cheered. But the other Sontarans were coming towards Karl. They were trying to point their guns at him.

'One day, Karl might save the world,' the Doctor said under his breath. Would it be today?

Another man ran out. The Doctor had seen him before. He had been in the one hundred metres sprint. He passed Karl, grabbing the sonic screwdriver like the baton in a relay race. Karl fell to his knees, and the laser beam flew over his head.

'Go Freddie!' yelled the crowd.

The Sontarans couldn't change the way they were going that quickly. By the time they were able to point their guns at Freddie, another sprinter had taken the screwdriver.

The runners were weaving their way across the arena. The trouble was, they were getting further and further away from the Doctor.

Then a voice called out of the crowd near the sprinters. Sid was hobbling down into the arena. 'To me!' he shouted.

The Sontarans were still trying to aim at the runner that had the sonic screwdriver. Karl had got up from the ground. He sprinted off again, and grabbed the screwdriver just in time. He hared towards the stands, and passed it to Sid.

Sid raised his arm. 'Holly, get down from there!' he called.

'I can't!' The girl was clinging to the force-sphere for dear life.

The Sontarans were heading for Sid. Their strides were getting heavier. Any second now, they would be able to aim at him.

The Doctor looked at Sid. He had grasped what was in the young javelin-thrower's mind.

Then he looked up at Holly. She was frozen with fear.

The Doctor felt a rush of guilt. He should never have asked someone with a head injury to climb so high.

He stood up straight. It was his fault, so he had to put it right.

'Sid, just do it!' he yelled.

Sid glanced at the Doctor, and nodded. He raised his arm and threw the sonic screwdriver, as if it were a tiny javelin.

The screwdriver flew into the air, higher and higher. Sid's aim was true. It hit the sphere's weak spot, dead on.

The crowd gasped.

Nothing happened.

'I set a 10-second delay!' shouted the Doctor.

He had started running almost before the sonic had left Sid's hand. The force-sphere hung over a spot more than a hundred metres away. He had ten seconds to get there.

If the Doctor made it in time, it would be a new world record.

He sprinted towards the spot. Lieutenant Skezz was still there, going round in circles. The Sontaran tried to aim his gun at the running Doctor.

He was nearly there...

There was a fizzing noise from above, and the force-sphere vanished.

The Doctor dodged the missiles as they rained down around him. He caught the falling Holly, and sped away.

The crowd cheered. They cheered even harder when a discus thumped onto the back of the spinning Skezz's neck. The Sontaran lay flat, still hanging just above the ground. Then all of a sudden, he fell to the floor with a crash.

'Their gravity's back to normal!'

The Doctor got to his feet, leaving Holly lying on the ground. Out of the corner of his eye he could see the students grabbing weapons.

But he was watching the Sontarans. Major Stenx, Captain Skeed and Lieutenant Slorr were all heading towards the young athletes. They were raising their guns.

'Sontarans!' yelled the Doctor, as loud as he could. 'I have won your Games! I am the victor! I demand the right to face you in combat! If you value your honour – face me now!'

The three aliens turned towards the Doctor. Their guns were pointing straight at him.

But now their backs were to the students.

About fifty missiles hit the Sontarans at once. Some bounced off the backs of their heads, or their armour, but enough found their mark.

Stenx, Skeed and Slorr fell, face down, onto the ground. They didn't stir.

The crowd went wild.

Chapter Fifteen

With the Sontarans out of the picture, the force shield vanished. A series of small pops came from the aliens' suits as controls short-circuited.

The Doctor tried the tunnel door and was pleased to find it was no longer sealed.

The athletes streamed back into BASE. Most didn't even pause to change, just headed straight out of the front door in their nightclothes. Karl and Sid both insisted on taking Holly to a hospital. The start of a beautiful friendship? Perhaps.

Soon the building was empty. Just the Doctor and the bodies remained.

There had been too many deaths. There were so many families who had been so proud, waiting to cheer on their loved ones at the Globe Games. There would be no medals now, just endless suffering.

The Doctor couldn't condone what the students had done, covering up the deaths. But he held on to the fact that they hadn't been the killers. He thought – hoped – things would be better now for them. They'd all learned what they could do when they worked together. Their future would be brighter than their past, whatever it held.

The Doctor went to check on the TARDIS. He needed to know he could get away. He hoped it didn't still have an electric charge running through it.

He found that the building wasn't empty after all. There was a young woman sitting on the floor by the TARDIS, where Jess's body had been. She was idly kicking the toolbox that still lay next to the ship.

'Hello,' said the Doctor.

'Hello,' said Emma.

The Doctor sat down next to her, crossing his legs.

'I'm glad you're not dead,' he said. 'I thought you would have left, though. The doors aren't sealed now.'

'I left the building,' she said. 'But I didn't have anywhere to go. So I came back to find you. Are you leaving? It's all sorted now.'

'Is it?' The Doctor looked at her. 'You've forgotten the people who died. Not just the ones killed by the Sontarans. The ones from earlier. Laura. Joe. Andy.'

'But the Sontarans killed them too!'

'Oh no they didn't.' The Doctor shook his head sadly. 'The Sontarans only arrived tonight. That was pretty clear from the way they acted. Anyway, Sontarans don't tend to electrocute people, despite what we saw in the arena. And talking of things electric, how about the electrician?' He reached out a booted foot and kicked the toolbox.

'The who?'

'The electrician. I wanted to know what Sid was doing, walking around down here late at night. He had to be quite close to hear you scream. No one else heard you. Sid thought I was an electrician. Then there was this toolbox and these special rubber boots. So when I had the chance, I asked him.'

Emma said nothing. She was biting her lip as the Doctor told his tale.

'Sid had sneaked out and called an electrician. He thought about calling the police, but he was worried because he'd helped to hush up the deaths. If an electrician could find out what was going on, though, then maybe no one else would die. That was his idea. He told the man to sneak in, and then came down to meet him last night. But someone had found him first. I wonder where his body is?'

Emma reached out and took a hammer from the toolbox.

The Doctor plucked it from her hand. 'I don't think so,' he said. 'You see, there's still one more death we have to talk about.' He looked into her eyes. 'The death of a young swimmer called Emma.'

The girl took a deep breath. 'How long have you known?'

'Oh, I've suspected it for a while. You gave yourself away – no big mistakes, but it was enough. You said you'd never seen the bodies, then you talked about seeing Laura floating in the pool. It was pretty clear you were up to something dodgy. It could have been anything, though.'

The Doctor sighed. 'But there was more. Lots more. The hand I found by the pool. The length of time you were able to stay underwater. I remembered how you'd asked about the Rutans. That threw me for a moment. But you just wanted to find out how much I knew. And I told you.'

He was still staring into her eyes. 'Except there were a few things I didn't mention at the time. Like how Rutans don't like heat – even heated swimming pools. And the big one. How they can absorb electricity, and use it to kill.'

Emma was hanging on his every word.

'And when I found out the Sontarans were looking for a shape-changer, that clinched it.' The Doctor looked at her sadly. 'You're the shape-changer. You're a Rutan.'

Chapter Sixteen

Emma nodded slowly.

'Why?' said the Doctor. 'Why come here in the first place? Did you crash-land?'

'Oh no.' Emma the Rutan shook her head. 'I was sent here. You see, the war's heading this way. We're going to need Earth soon. But it takes time to form a base on an inhabited planet. Wiping out the natives can be costly, too. Much better to get them to do it for you.'

The Doctor didn't like what he was hearing. 'You wanted the humans to wipe themselves out?'

'That was the plan. The Globe Games are a world event. Many of Earth's nations are on the brink of war. If I was part of the Games, I could push them over that brink.'

'A scandal here, a murder there?' asked the Doctor.

'That sort of thing. So I was sent here to BASE. I could have waited for the Games themselves...'

'... but you wanted to practise being human

first,' the Doctor said. He was almost enjoying himself, seeing all the pieces of the puzzle fall into place. 'As Rutans are used to being in the water, you decided to become a swimmer. You hid at the pool until someone came along on their own. The real Emma. You killed her. Then you took her body apart. You needed to do that to find out how it worked, so you could copy it yourself.'

'Human bodies are very complex,' the Rutan agreed. 'Even when I'd mastered the shape, it took some time to copy the movement. I was found by the human girl Laura. She joined me in the pool, thinking I was Emma. I found out much from her. But she saw I was not swimming in the human way. She knew something was wrong. Then she spotted one of Emma's hands that I had not disposed of. She began to scream.'

'So you killed her. Sucked all the electricity out of the building, and zapped her with it. The first power cut.' The Doctor spoke in a matter-of-fact way, to hide how he was really feeling. 'Before hiding poor dead Emma's hand down a grating.'

'Yes. After that, I was ready. I filled myself with electricity before I tried to swim. That way, I could protect myself if anyone found me.'

'You didn't stop at two deaths. Did Laura's boyfriend suspect something? What about Joe the sprinter?'

'He was just in the wrong place at the wrong time. Then I saw the electrician poking around as I was on my way to the pool. I knew I would have to get rid of him. It was a close thing, though. I had to wait until he'd taken off his silly boots. I couldn't shock him while he was wearing those.' She laughed. 'Talking of shocks – guess how I felt when your ship appeared!'

The Doctor stood up and turned to face the TARDIS. He hadn't really looked at it since he'd landed. First there had been the power cut, then it had been electrified.

He walked round to the back of the police box. There was only a small gap between the ship and the wall. It was just big enough to hold the body of the electrician. He had been a short, dark-skinned man with black curly hair and a tiny moustache.

'I electrified your ship to stop you finding him,' the Rutan Emma said, joining him. 'Well, partly that. I would be put to death if I left without completing my mission, and I needed your help. To defeat the Sontarans, I mean. I didn't think you'd help me wipe out the humans.' She laughed.

The Doctor didn't laugh. He wasn't finding any of this funny.

'I have a question too,' she went on.

'Oh yes?'

'If you've known for so long that I'm not Emma the human, why didn't you say something before?'

This time the Doctor did laugh. 'Because I'm a fool!' he said. 'I thought you might be trying to change. You were helping me. Oh, I know you just wanted me to defeat the Sontarans for you, but you were still helping. At times, you seemed to show concern for the humans here. Helping Holly when she was hurt, that sort of thing.'

He paused and looked sadly at her. 'I thought if I treated you kindly, you might realise that my way is better. You might stop the killing. For a moment, I even thought you'd given your life for us all. No human could have survived what happened to you in the arena. Then I realised that you could just absorb the power.'

'If you'd looked up, you would have seen me in my own body,' she told him. 'I hadn't got a grip on being Emma again. You see, I'd shifted into Sontaran form to get out of the gym. One of them nearly found me when I was talking to you through the cupboard door. Luckily, we

94

shape-changing elite are made to learn Sontaran as a default form.'

'Lucky for me, I suppose,' the Doctor agreed.

'The blast made me revert to my own body, then launched me right across the arena. I stayed out of sight until it was all over. You didn't need my help any more. You could deal with the Sontarans yourself.' She smiled at him.

The Doctor didn't smile back. 'And now what? We all live happily ever after?'

'Well, why not?'

'Because I don't know if you have changed. You don't seem sorry that you've killed six people here. Emma. Laura. Andy. Joe. Jess. The electrician. Do you still plan to win Earth for the Rutans?'

'They would kill me if I did not,' she said.

The Doctor shook his head. 'Not if I took you away from here in the TARDIS. I could give you a second chance.'

There was a flash of green light. The Doctor flung up his hands to shield his eyes. When he could see again, Emma had gone. In the girl's place was a large green jelly-like blob, pulsing with white veins. Hairy white fronds floated from its body, like a beard made of seaweed.

'Showing your true colours?' the Doctor asked. 'Mainly green, I see.'

The Rutan spoke. It was no longer using Emma's voice, the sound it made was low and grating. 'I could kill you and take your craft,' it said.

The light bulb hanging from the ceiling flickered, and energy crackled across the alien's skin.

'I think I could learn to fly it,' the Rutan went on. 'My mission would be easy with a time ship. My people would reward me for it.'

The Doctor waved a booted foot in the air. 'Just try it,' he said. 'You can't give me any deadly shocks while I've got my special rubber boots on! Now come on. What's it going to be? This is your last chance to take your last chance.'

He braced himself, not sure that even the boots would protect him if the alien attacked. But the Rutan seemed to be thinking about his words. The green glow within its huge round body went darker, then became lighter again. 'I...' it said slowly. 'I...'

'Death to Rutans!'

The shout came from the doorway. The Doctor spun round. Major Stenx staggered into the room. The broken tip of a javelin was still sticking out of his probic vent. The Doctor couldn't believe the Sontaran was still alive.

'Sontaran!' The Rutan was rushing across the

room towards its enemy. The lights went out, but the Doctor could still see. Tendrils of power whipped around the Rutan's body, lighting up the room.

'I give you a death you do not deserve!' cried Stenx. 'You will die in battle, with honour!'

'It is you who will die!' the Rutan replied.

Major Stenx pointed his wand-like gun at the Rutan and fired. Beam after beam of red light hit the crackling green Rutan blob.

Power snaked from the Rutan. A line of energy hit the broken piece of metal that had stuck in the Sontaran's neck. All of BASE's energy was poured into Stenx's weak spot.

Green blood began to bubble from the major's mouth. 'I... die... in...battle!' he gasped, as he fell to his knees. A second later, he lay on the floor. Dead.

But it wasn't over yet.

Sparks began to shoot from Stenx's body. The Doctor turned to the Rutan. 'You have to contain the power!'

There was no answer. The Doctor looked closer. Stenx's laser beams had hit their target too many times. The Rutan – he couldn't help still thinking of it as 'Emma' – was dead too. But, somehow, it was still sucking power from BASE, and pouring it into the Sontaran.

The Doctor needed to get out of there, and fast. He clicked his fingers and the TARDIS doors swung open.

'Who needs a key?' he said.

It was the work of a moment to take off. He looked at the scanner as he did so, just in time to see a massive flash of white light. The whole building had exploded. Well, at least that would tie up any loose ends. No alien bodies to be found.

The Doctor thought back to that last body, the green blob slowly folding in on itself.

'I wish I knew what you'd decided, Emma,' he whispered. 'I don't offer second chances very often. I think... I think we might have given each other another chance.'

He turned away from the scanner, and began to set the controls. He had other places to visit. Other lives to save.

With a sad smile, he corrected himself. Other lives to *try to* save.

All he could do was his best.

Quick Reads

Books in the Quick Reads series

Quick Reads

Pick up a book today

Quick Reads are bite-sized books by bestselling writers and well-known personalities for people who want a short, fast-paced read. They are designed to be read and enjoyed by avid readers and by people who never had or who have lost the reading habit.

Quick Reads are published alongside and in partnership with BBC RaW.

We would like to thank all our partners in the Quick Reads project for their help and support:

Arts Council England
The Department for Innovation, Universities and Skills
NIACE
unionlearn
National Book Tokens
The Vital Link
The Reading Agency
National Literacy Trust
Welsh Books Council
Basic Skills Cymru, Welsh Assembly Government
Wales Accent Press
The Big Plus Scotland
DELNI
NALA

Quick Reads would also like to thank the Department for Innovation, Universities and Skills; Arts Council England and World Book Day for their sponsorship and NIACE for their outreach work.

Quick Reads is a World Book Day initiative.
www.quickreads.org.uk   www.worldbookday.com

Quick Reads

Doctor Who: I Am a Dalek
Gareth Roberts

BBC Books

Equipped with space suits, golf clubs and a flag, the Doctor and Rose are planning to live it up on the Moon, Apollo-mission style. But the TARDIS has other plans, landing them instead in a village on the south coast of England; a picture-postcard sort of place where nothing much happens... until now.

Archaeologists have dug up a Roman mosaic, dating from the year 70 AD. It shows scenes from ancient myths, bunches of grapes – and a Dalek. A few days later a young woman, rushing to get to work, is knocked over and killed by a bus. Then she comes back to life.

It's not long before all hell breaks loose, and the Doctor and Rose must use all their courage and cunning against an alien enemy – and a not-quite-alien accomplice – who are intent on destroying humanity.

Featuring the Doctor and Rose as played by David Tennant and Billie Piper in the hit series from BBC Television.

Quick Reads

Doctor Who: Made of Steel
Terrance Dicks

BBC Books

A deadly night attack on an army base. Vehicles are destroyed, soldiers killed. The attackers vanish as swiftly as they came, taking highly advanced equipment with them.

Metal figures attack a shopping mall. But why do they only want a new games console from an ordinary electronics shop? An obscure government ministry is blown up – but, in the wreckage, no trace is found of the secret, state-of-the-art decoding equipment.

When the TARDIS returns the Doctor and Martha to Earth from a distant galaxy, they try to piece together the mystery. But someone – or something – is waiting for them. An old enemy stalks the night, men no longer made of flesh...

Featuring the Doctor and Martha as played by David Tennant and Freema Agyeman in the hit series from BBC Television.

Quick Reads

Doctor Who: Revenge of the Judoon
Terrance Dicks

BBC Books

The TARDIS brings the Doctor and Martha to Balmoral in 1902. Here they meet Captain Harry Carruthers – friend of the new king, Edward VII. Together they head for the castle to see the king – only to find that Balmoral Castle has gone, leaving just a hole in the ground. The Doctor realises it is the work of the Judoon – a race of ruthless space police.

While Martha and Carruthers seek answers in London, the Doctor finds himself in what should be the most deserted place on Earth – and he is not alone.

Featuring the Doctor and Martha as played by David Tennant and Freema Agyeman in the hit series from BBC Television.

Other resources

Free courses are available for anyone who wants to develop their skills. You can attend the courses in your local area. If you'd like to find out more, phone 0800 66 0800.

Don't get by get on 0800 66 0800

A list of books for new readers can be found on www. firstchoicebooks.org.uk or at your local library.

The
Vital
Link

Publishers Barrington Stoke (www.barringtonstoke.co.uk), New Island (www.newisland.ie) and Sandstone Press (www.sandstonepress.com) also provide books for new readers.

Barrington Stoke

OPEN DOOR

SANDSTONE PRESS
CONTEMPORARY QUALITY READING

The BBC runs a reading and writing campaign. See www.bbc.co.uk/raw.

RaW